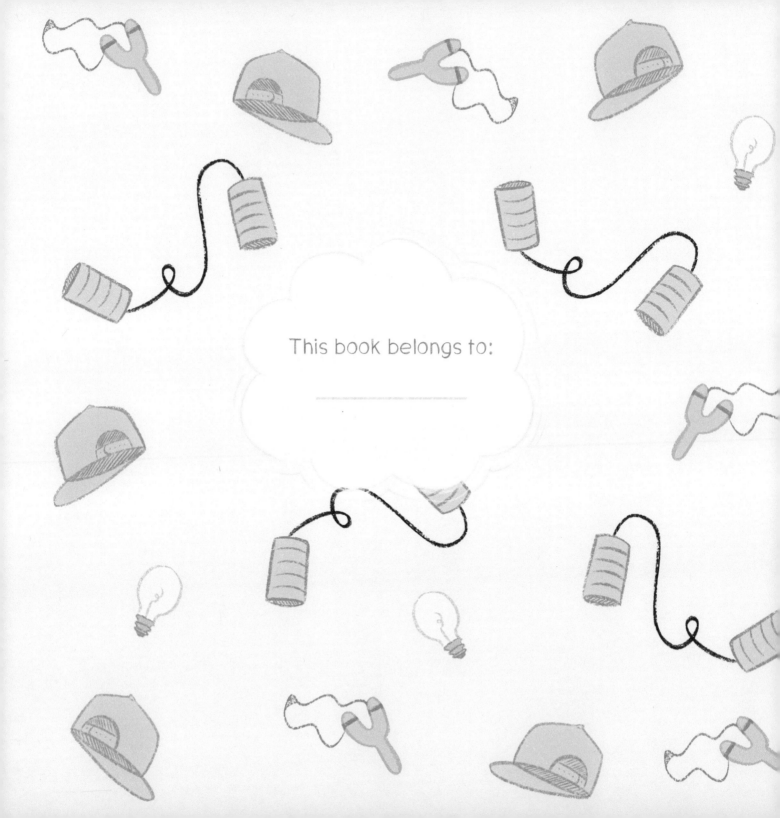

This book belongs to:

_____

Kaden, Brendon, and Rhett

Butt chins
ROCK
and so do you!

Publisher's Cataloging-in-Publication data

Names: Curren, Ashly, author. | Hruska, Danielle, illustrator.
Title: A what chin? / Ashly Curren ; illustrated by Danielle Hruska.
Description: Indianapolis, IN: Ashly Curren, 2020. |
Summary: After being told he has a butt chin - a little boy takes
drastic measures to get rid of it. Will he succeed?

Identifiers:
LCCN: 2020909973
ISBN: 978-1-7351565-1-4 (Hardcover)
       978-1-7351565-2-1 (pbk.)
       978-1-7351565-0-7 (ebook)

Subjects: LCSH Face--Juvenile fiction. | Bullying--Juvenile fiction.
Self-esteem--Juvenile fiction. | CYAC Face--Fiction. | Bullying--Fiction.
Self-esteem--Fiction. | BISAC JUVENILE FICTION / Social Themes / Bullying
JUVENILE FICTION / Social Themes / Self-Esteem & Self-Reliance
Classification: LCC PZ7.1 C8648 Wha 2020 | DDC [E]--dc23

a WHAT chin?

written by
Ashly Curren

illustrated by
Danielle Hruska

A WHAT chin did I hear them say?

I want to make it CLEAR.

A <u>BUTT</u> chin?

Yes, you heard it too!

Oh
DEAR,

oh
DEAR,

oh
DEAR!

They said I have a
BUTT CHIN,
but...

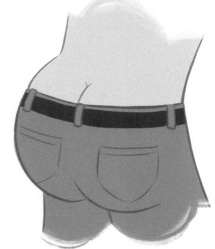

I think that's truly RUDE.

It
doesn't
FART...

...or
BOTHER
them.

My mommy thinks it's kinda cute.

I get it from
MY DAD.

How DARE they call my chin a butt?

Why must they be
SO BAD?

I know a lot of people who
have chins that look
LIKE MINE,
and I would never call them names.

I think they look
JUST
FINE.

So how can I be HAPPY with a problem on my CHIN?

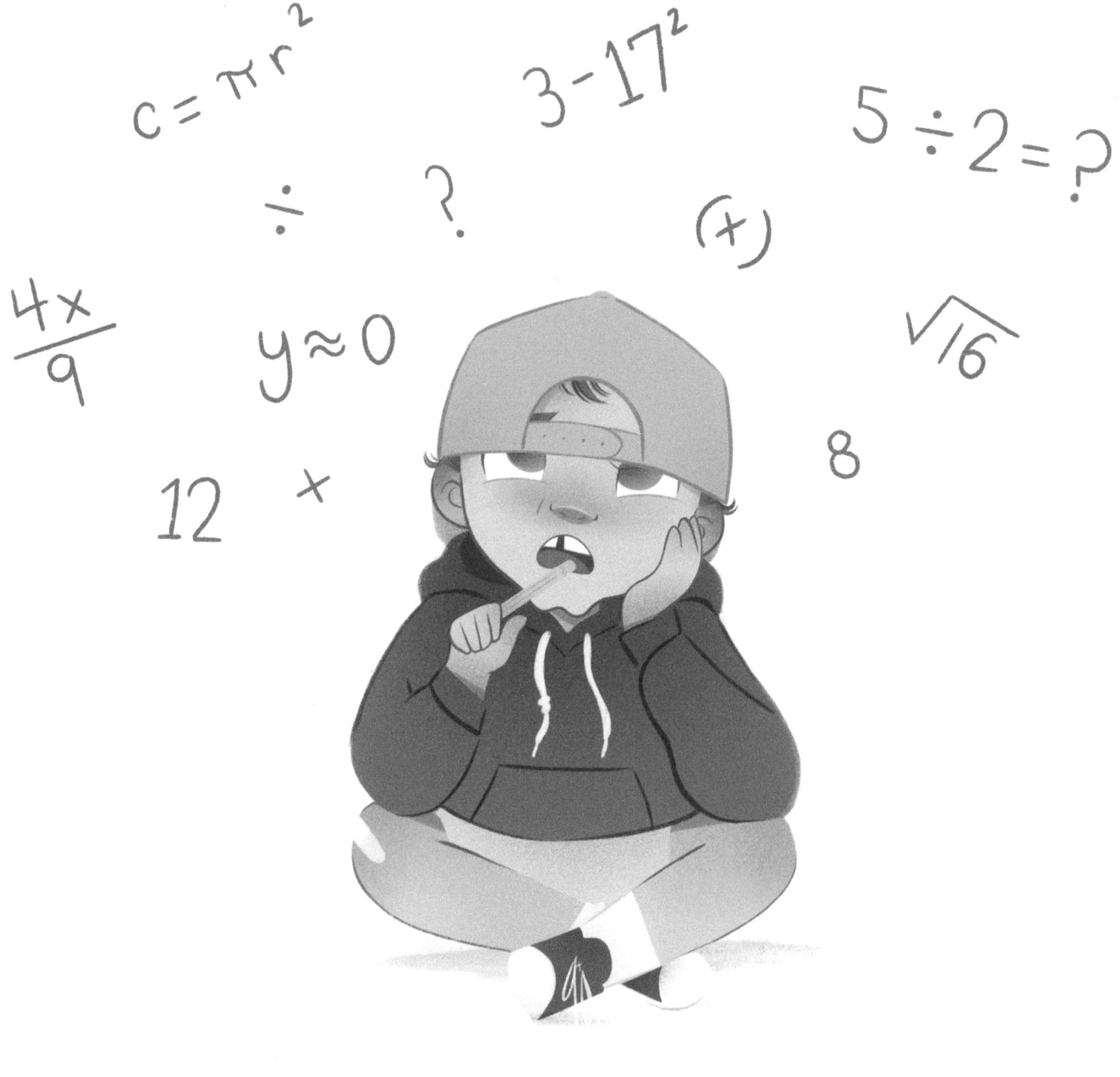

My dad says,
"Son, you need to know,

you're
PERFECT
from within."

"Those kids just may be jealous,
and perhaps they're insecure.
Don't let them make you sad, my son.
You're HANDSOME, to be sure!"

"We all have imperfections,
so don't let them get you down.
Just own your chin. It makes you YOU.
Don't let them make
you frown."

But dad just doesn't get it...
I don't want a
STINKY
CHIN!

So maybe I can
WISH
it gone,

Or
PLUCK
IT
OFF
my skin.

Or maybe I can
grow a
BEARD!

Hey, that would bring a scare.

And maybe that would hide my face.

This life just isn't FAIR!

And prove that my ole butt chin

Can be
TOOTED
out
of
place.

That's bound to really show them, and I **CAN'T STOP** laughing now.

It could shoot right off MY FACE...

To outer space—

KA-POW!

To fart my chin right off my face
is filling me
with GLEE.

If I could really pull that off,
I know I would
feel FREE.

But that's okay, I'm cool now.

My chin's more fun than theirs.

My special chin is too UNIQUE!

If they make fun,
WHO CARES?

Lightning Source UK Ltd.
Milton Keynes UK
UKHW051257011220
374405UK00002B/26